For my Mum and Dad

First published 2018 by Walker Books Ltd,
87 Vauxhall Walk, London SE11 5HJ

10 9 8 7 6 5 4 3 2 1

© 2018 Jane McGuinness

This book has been set in VAG rounded

Printed in China

British Library Cataloguing in Publication Data:
a catalogue record for this book is available
from the British Library

ISBN 978-1-4063-7460-5

www.walker.co.uk

Say Hi to Hedgehogs!

Jane McGuinness

WALKER BOOKS
AND SUBSIDIARIES
LONDON · BOSTON · SYDNEY · AUCKLAND

Do you hear that? Listen.

Someone's **sniffling** and **snuffling**
and **snaffling** ...

whirring and churring and purring

... making a lovely racket!

Someone small and spiky.

Hi, Hedgehog!

HUFF!

snort!

Hedgehog's spikes are called prickles, and they're made from the same stuff as your fingernails. When she feels calm and relaxed, Hedgehog lays her prickles down flat – then she's safe to touch.

A hedgehog can have up to 5,000 prickles. Each prickle lasts about a year before it falls out and a new one grows in its place.

But if she's stressed or frightened,
be careful! Her prickles stand up on end,
and she rolls into a tight ball.

Hedgehogs curl up into a ball to protect their
soft bellies from predators.

Hedgehogs are "nocturnal".
That means they sleep all day and
usually only come out at night.

When the sun has set and you're tucked
up in bed, Hedgehog's day has only just started.
She's out and about, pushing through the undergrowth
as she searches for things to eat.

sharp

Hedgehogs have bright little
eyes, but in the dark their
sharp noses are much more
useful for sniffing out food.

Hedgehog snuffles
her way home to
her nest, which is
hidden in a safe, quiet
place. Her babies are
snug and warm inside
– she feeds and cleans
them, then they curl
up together to sleep.

Baby hedgehogs are called
"hoglets"; a group of hoglets is called
a "litter". Usually there are around
five hoglets to a litter.

Hoglets drink their mother's milk until they are ready to eat solid food.

Hoglets are pink, bald, blind and deaf when they're born, and their prickles are soft and white.

13

After a few weeks the hoglets have grown their fur and teeth, and their prickles have become tougher. They follow Hedgehog on short walks outside the nest.

Hedgehog teaches her hoglets
how to hunt in just ten days.

15

Soon they're ready to find their own way
in the big, wide world.

The hoglets climb over branches and scrabble under hedgerows, each
one searching for somewhere to make a new home.

They need luck on their side because there are all kinds
of dangers out there, like busy roads and hungry badgers.

This little hedgehog heads for the park –
a good place to find food.

He might be small, but Little Hedgehog has a big appetite.

Sometimes he walks a whole mile in a night ...

sniff-sniff-sniffing for things to eat.

Hedgehogs have surprisingly
long legs: at top speed,
they can run as fast
as we can walk.

Little Hedgehog's favourite foods are probably not the same as yours!

Flies

Woodlice

Moths

Slugs and snails

Spiders

Ants

Worms

20

Hedgehogs mostly eat worms, slugs, insects and spiders, but they sometimes eat birds' eggs, frogs, fish and fruit, as well.

Millipedes

Grasshoppers

Butterflies

Bugs and beetles

Centipedes

Little Hedgehog eats and eats and eats,

through the summer and right into the autumn.

A hedgehog needs to weigh 600 g to survive the winter – about the same as a football.

He's getting fatter and fatter – ready for winter when there isn't as much food around.

At the end of autumn Little Hedgehog makes a nest of his own.

He gathers dry leaves, bendy twigs and soft moss,

piling them up and up until his nest is strong and warm.

When the weather
turns colder, and
Little Hedgehog
has a full,
round stomach,
it is time to curl up
in his cosy bed.

Hedgehogs sleep all winter long: this is called "hibernation".
While they hibernate hedgehogs slowly burn energy, using
the fat stores they have built up over the summer.

Goodnight, Little Hedgehog.

See you in spring!

Making Your Home Hedgehog-Friendly

There used to be hedgehogs all over the country but now there are far fewer around, so it's important to do everything we can to keep them safe. It can be difficult for town hedgehogs to get from garden to garden, so try making small holes in your fences and hedges to create a hedgehog highway. If you have a garden pond, be sure to put some kind of ramp at the edge (a small piece of wood is perfect) so that any hedgehogs who go for a swim can climb safely out.

You could also try leaving out food and water (hedgehogs prefer meaty things, like cat food), or making a hedgehog shelter. Hedgehogs nest in dark, cosy places, so make sure to check leaf piles and unlit bonfires for their nests before you disturb them. If you ever happen across a hedgehog nest, gently replace any leaves or twigs and leave it alone.

If you find a hedgehog who needs help, contact the **British Hedgehog Preservation Society** or your local wildlife organisation – they'll have plenty of tips and advice.

Index

Look up the pages to find out about all these hedgehoggy things. Don't forget to look up both kinds of word – **this kind** and *this kind*.

Books:

Morgan, Sally (2005), *British Wildlife: Hedgehogs*,
London: Franklin Watts.

Warwick, Hugh (2010), *A Prickly Affair:
The Charm of the Hedgehog*,
London: Penguin.

Websites:

British Hedgehog Preservation Society
www.britishhedgehogs.org.uk

Hedgehog Street
www.hedgehogstreet.org

Tiggywinkles
www.sttiggywinkles.org.uk

Prickles Hedgehog Rescue
www.prickleshedgehogrescue.org.uk

Wildlife Trusts
www.wildlifetrusts.org/hedgehogs

RSPCA
www.rspca.org.uk/adviceandwelfare/
wildlife/inthewild/gardenhedgehogs

RSPB
www.rspb.org.uk/get-involved/
community-and-advice/garden-advice/
homes_for_mammals/hedgehogs.aspx